SPECIAL RELATIVITY IN SPACE

A HAYWARD HALL SHORT STORY

ALEXANDRIA BLAELOCK

BlueMere Books
MELBOURNE, AUSTRALIA

For permission requests, please contact
enquiries@bluemerebooks.com.

Ordering Information:
Discounts are available on quantity purchases. For details, contact orders@bluemerebooks.com.

Special Relativity in Space/Alexandria Blaelock
paperback ISBN: 978-1-925749-62-5
digital ISBN: 978-1-925749-63-2

Book Layout © BookDesignTemplates.com

SPECIAL RELATIVITY IN SPACE

S pace Mariner third class Kumahl Levi worked in a small cubicle.

It was a fairly standard ship cubicle, supplied with a small view screen capable of showing all of the cargo holds, and with his login, nothing else.

The communication system permitted ship-to-ship and ship-wide internal communications, but only private messages to the section heads.

Access to the ship's mainframe computer was only that required for the conduct of transport operations and nothing further.

The cubicle included a slightly broken black chair, and not enough elbow room.

Personal items were not permitted, so the grey cubicle was as blank, pristine and boring as the day it was made.

Only slightly more worn.

Thanks to his placement aboard the *AESV Albatross* he was working ship time; scheduled 6 hours on/12 hours off, instead of the 8/16 he'd be working in a placement back on Earth.

For the most part, his work was tedious and monotonous; he sat in his cubicle watching the transport panel.

And as he was the most junior transport officer, working through the "night" didn't help.

Thanks to the barely detectable hum and vibration of the engines, the slightly too warm temperature and the close, re breathed ship atmosphere, his tiny workspace was soporific. Only the occasional flash of a light or ping of an alarm to keep him awake.

And of course, most of the interesting work, like pulling apart the transporter mechanisms, and performing routine maintenance happened during the "swing".

With one hour of his watch left, there was one ship-to-ship transport scheduled.

Thankfully no training, and hopefully, no emergency drills during his "off" shift.

Now and again, he adjusted the wavelengths or time compensators and noted the calculations in the logs.

Or triggered automatic recalibrations.

Or a manual one for something a bit different.

All the major repairs and refits were done in the ship yard, so precious little of that to do.

There hadn't been a serious incident this tour, but he was so bored he almost wanted some kind of emergency situation.

Despite the monstrous amount paperwork that would require.

As if on cue, a burst of static heralded the transport.

"*AESV Albatross* this is *AESV Mermaid*, do you read?"

"Yes *Mermaid*, I read you."

"I have one standard container to transfer."

"I can receive one standard container. You have permission to enter the loading zone."

"Confirmed. Please prepare *Albatross* for loading."

"*Mermaid*, I can receive in five minutes on my mark," Kumahl set a stopwatch for five minutes and ten seconds, and at five seconds he started counting down.

"Five. Four. Three. Two."

"Mark," they said together.

"*Albatross*, I am sending the cargo manifest."

After a short pause, Kumahl confirmed, "I have received the manifest."

The transport appeared in the loading bay as expected, so he started the contamination scans.

"*Mermaid*, I have received your transport, and am initiating scans."

"I understand."

And that's where it started getting complicated.

The biohazard warning flashed and pinged, and for something to while away the last few minutes of his shift, he ran a detailed analysis to determine the hazard rather than just venting the atmosphere to destroy it.

And that's where it started getting puzzling.

Because the biohazard was human.

And if the analysis was correct, a human female.

A living human female.

Alone.

In deep space.

Well, not deep space exactly, but a vacuum sealed shipping container, that shouldn't in theory, contain humans.

According to interstellar law, all ships had a clear duty to help those in distress in space.

And there had been recent reports of human smuggling to the outer colonies.

And this was an Allied Earth Shipping Vessel...

He sent alarms to security and deckhands, an alert to the Captain and hailed the other ship.

"AESV *Mermaid*, this is AESV *Albatross*, do you read me."

"Yes *Albatross*, I read you."

"The shipping container includes a human female that is not in the cargo manifest."

"Say again please."

"Your shipping container includes a human female, not in the manifest."

"Kumahl are you pranking me?"

"No Seth. Unless there is an error in the scanning, a human is in the container."

"Confirmed. I will seek further information. Please stand by."

Internally, a security squad in protective suits arrived in the cargo hold and held a buzz of backward and forward comms with the dockworkers.

Kumahl knew it was there, but couldn't hear it.

He watched them preparing to break into the container.

As security stood, weapons at the ready, the dock workers brought in the heavy-duty laser cutters, cut through the lock, and opened the doors.

There was a pause; presumably security was demanding an orderly exit of the container.

A woman walked out with her hands up.

She wasn't wearing a ship suit, but weirdly in this day and age, an old-fashioned ankle length dress.

With what looked like lace on it.

An armed officer darted forward to secure her for the medical check and further interrogation.

"*Albatross*, I can confirm the woman was not detected in the departure scan. Are you sure there's one there?"

"I can confirm. I am looking at her."

"I will send you the scan."

After a couple of minutes, Kumahl confirmed, "I have received the scans."

He ran a quick eye over the scans, "I will seek further information. Please stand by."

He copied the information to the Captain, requesting departure clearance for the *Mermaid*.

It seemed an open and shut case.

The woman was not in the container when it left, and was somehow beamed in during the transfer.

It was an enormous risk; if the calculations were off by a fraction of a second, she'd be floating dead in the vacuum of space.

You had to admire that level of precision.

He watched as she was escorted from the cargo hold and the Captain returned permission to depart.

"*Mermaid* you are cleared to depart."

"I am underway. Let me know what happens with your mystery human."

"Will do. *Albatross* out."

And that was the end of the matter as far as Space Mariner third class Kumahl Levi was concerned.

He logged the activity of the day as far as transport was concerned, and closed out his station ready for the next shift transport officer.

Greater minds than him would look at how the woman had achieved the transport.

It was an interesting mystery, and he looked forward to reading the reports.

Assuming they weren't classified.

In the meantime, he was off shift, and after that level of excitement, he needed a beer.

Or two.

《《 • 》》

Morag Clementine understood the need for security.

After all, as far as they were concerned, she'd just materialised out of nowhere.

But did they have to be quite so rough?

And tie the restraints quite so tight?

And literally throw her in the brig?

At least that what she assumed this cold featureless room was.

It was all smooth metallic grey, like brushed steel - floors, walls, ceiling. The joints between the walls and the floor and ceiling were featureless, concave surfaces.

It was disorienting, like being in a grey bubble.

There was no where to sit, or lie down, and nothing to do.

She'd always considered herself a law-abiding citizen, and for the most part, leaving aside a few pirated TV shows, smoked joints and occasional speeding, had always done the right thing.

That an armed squad who was so impolite as to be considered rude was in charge of her had come as quite a shock.

On top of what had already been a full day, she was exhausted.

She'd got married that morning, phase shifted in the afternoon, and now, teleported into a shipping container in the evening.

To say it had been a full day was an understatement.

She was about dead on her feet, and expecting her day to get worse, so she curled up on the floor and took a nap.

It seemed she'd just dozed off when she was woken by a hiss of gas in the room.

For an instant she imagined something like Zyklon B, but after a few moments of not choking, was reassured.

Perhaps it was reasonable of the guys in sealed suits to assume she was a carrier of something.

Not that she knew anything about the ship, but as an Australian, was aware of the disastrous consequences of injudicious imports; cane toads, foxes and Indian myna birds to name a few.

Not to mention quarantine breaches like fire ants, European Wasps and Mediterranean Fruit Fly.

There was definitely a great deal to be said for biosecurity controls.

Or offshore detention for asylum seekers, but that was a different kind of security concern, one she didn't agree with.

The gas had barely stopped hissing before waves of coloured lasers bathed the room from top to bottom, and bottom to top.

She felt a tiny pinprick, like an insect bite, and rubbed her arm as the lasers ceased their display and the fog was sucked back out of the room.

After a while she gave up her expectation of immediate action, and went back to sleep.

Kumahl was woken early by a crewman with orders to attend the Captain's ready room.

Immediately.

Not that you ever really changed into pyjamas during a tour so that wasn't a problem.

But he had to prepare the bed for the next watch, splash water on his face and brush his teeth which took a little more time than immediately.

No time for coffee before scuttling down the passageways either.

All too soon he was knocking on a door, waiting for permission to enter.

"Enter."

Kumahl straightened his uniform hat, pulled his tunic down, and took a deep breath.

He opened the door, shut the door, took two paces forward and saluted the Captain.

She was standing at the map table with two women and a man.

Going by the uniform insignia, three officers, perhaps even her Command Executives.

"At ease," she said.

Kumahl relaxed, spread his legs a little and folded his hands together in front of his hips.

"Levi, I understand you have some knowledge of temporal effects on subatomic particles?"

He was puzzled by the question, "my Doctoral dissertation was on the astrophysical effects of long-term gravitational time dilation on subatomic particle cohesiveness Sir."

"And I understand Professor Smythe was impressed by your innovative treatment of gravitational time dilation?"

Curiouser and curiouser.

"Ah, yes Sir."

"And you co-wrote a paper that is still debated in academic circles?"

"Er, yes, but I'm not sure…"

The Captain glanced at each member of the group, and they nodded back.

"Let me introduce you to Chief Medical Officer Yang," she said, pointing him out on her left.

"Security Chief Singh," the woman in the centre.

"And Chief of Logistics McMasters," the woman on the right.

Kumahl stepped his feet back together, and saluted each in turn. They nodded back.

He relaxed again, curiosity eating him alive.

"We've been discussing the young woman from the shipping container," the Captain continued.

"Doctor Yang says she's in good health, and not a biothreat to the crew.

"Chief Singh has run a DNA scan, and she's not in any known database. Ordinarily we'd conclude she's a separatist, therefore suspect her motives in getting on board the *Albatross*.

"But Chief McMasters, has detected anomalies in her subatomic particles, and we're not sure what that means right now."

Kumahl nodded, but didn't say anything, though he had an idea where this was going.

"We'd like you to talk to the woman, who claims to be from 1905, see what you make of her story and come back to us on this."

"Yes Sir."

"Now, we don't want this getting out into the crew."

"No Sir."

"So until the situation is resolved, we're relieving you from transport duty, and explaining this as punishment for bringing an undocumented traveller on board."

"Yes Sir."

She smiled, "you will of course be working first shift for this project, and will report regularly to me.

"Yes Sir."

"Now," she checked her watch, "she should be about done with the quarantine protocols in pod one, why don't you escort her to Medical Observation Suite Four and organise breakfast for her?"

"Yes Sir."

"For the duration, we've allocated science lab two for you to work in."

It was the small, reputedly out-of-date lab.

The least visited, and the most out of the way lab.

And now he finally understood it was for secret projects

"Yes Sir," he saluted and left the room before they could change their minds.

But as he made his way down the passageways to quarantine pod one, he was jubilant enough to do a little dance.

Well, finally, something worth saying in his personal log.

And finally, his dissertation had some real-world repercussions.

It was kinda what he'd gone into space for.

But as he stood outside the pod, he became nervous.

What would this woman from the past be like? Did he need to be extra sensitive?

He knocked on the door, waited a moment, then opened it.

She had shoulder length red hair, and green eyes, and possibly freckles.

It was hard to say under the layer of dirt she and her dress were wearing.

She'd been trying to put her hair in order, and he'd caught her with her hands in her hair.

Trying to look nonchalant, she brushed some dust from the skirt of her dress.

"Hello," he said, "I'm Kumahl. I'm here to escort you to your temporary quarters."

She cocked her head at him, mimicking the sounds he'd made, and he realised she didn't understand Earth Standard.

He tried again in Earth English, "I'm Kumahl. I'm here to escort you to your temporary quarters."

Her face brightened, "I'm Morag. I don't suppose there's somewhere there to freshen up?"

"Freshen up?"

"Ah, this is going to be fun. Bathe"

As she saw his frown, she tried again, "Wash?"

"Shower?"

"Ah, I understand, there is a private cleaning cubicle in the room. Please come with me."

He left the room, and she followed, craning her neck up and down to see everything.

Pausing as they passed corridors, presumably noting the lack of other people.

"I don't want to seen ungrateful, but is there food in there as well?"

"There is not, but I will get you some."

They stopped at a door that looked very much like any other, and he opened it.

Inside, the room was spacious by ship standards, being roughly equivalent to a junior officer's room.

The single bed, dressed in white linens with a blue blanket rested on a set of drawers, one of them slightly open to reveal a ship suit.

At right angles to the bed, a drawer unit incorporated a fold down table, with a chair currently tucked under the table.

Next to that, a small upright locker, containing the sink, toilet facilities and shower.

The walls, furniture, ceiling, as well as the warren of pipes attached to the ceiling were painted cream to reflect the one light housed in the ceiling.

Morag looked dismayed, and Kumahl hasted to reassure her, "this is spacious compared to mine."

"Really?"

"Yes, I have a berth I share with two others and one small locker."

"Actually, I was looking at the shower unit."

"Ah, well, it's small, but it's all yours. You won't be sharing it with a third of the crew complement. And it allows us to monitor your medical state."

"I see. And am I a prisoner here?"

"Not a prisoner, but not at liberty to leave until we've managed the risks associated with you being here.

"For you, as well as for us."

"I understand. Like when the Spanish brought smallpox to Mexico and decimated the Incan empire."

He puzzled through her language for a moment, and then said, "exactly. Or in this instance, more that we infect you."

"I'll leave you to bathe, and will return with breakfast."

«« • »»

Morag took a quick, and uncomfortable shower, and dressed in the ship suit.

It was like one of those pairs of active socks that are too tight when you first put them on, but adjust as your body warms the fibres up.

It was quite form-fitting, and having become accustomed to dressing in looser, less revealing clothes over the last year, she felt quite exposed.

She crossed her fingers and washed out her dress and underthings, hoping whatever the detergent was wouldn't ruin the dress because it had cost a fortune.

And it was her wedding dress.

And by the time she was done, Kumahl was knocking on the door. She raced to open it before he could let himself in.

Which was just as well, because he'd brought food. Something that looked like eggs, toasted bread, and some kind of salad. With a knife and fork.

And something that smelled like coffee, and tasted divine.

She didn't dare ask if any of it was fresh or recycled; she just pretended it was fresh.

Even though she new it probably wasn't.

"Do you have a computer with whatever the Internet looks like tight now?" she asked, sitting at the desk and tucking into the eggs.

"I'm pretty sure computers didn't come about until the late twentieth century."

She looked up absently as she munched. "No, I think my parents got their first computer in the late 1980s."

"But if you come from 1905 as you claim?"

"Ah, I see where you're going. It's a long story."

"I have plenty of time," he said, sitting on the bed and pulling a phone out his pocket.

Which was disappointing because she was expecting something a bit more Trekish.

Attempting to martial her thoughts, she picked up the coffee mug, and tucking her hand through the handle, cradled it in both hands.

"Right then." She took a sip of the coffee, "it was 2020 when I took a job at Hayward Hall in Melbourne. The Australian Melbourne.

"I met Henry Fox at the Hall. He and the Master Suite were trapped in some kind of time space loop on September 9th, 1904.

"Every day he woke up in a different time and place, but couldn't get back through the bedroom door."

He nodded as she got up, typing into his phone, thumbs flying. She picked up a piece of toast, and started pacing the room.

"I did some research, and I thought it was something to do with the lunar eclipse in conjunction with a low-pressure system and maybe a thunderstorm."

He nodded again, still tapping away.

On her way back she picked up the coffee again.

"On the 25th of November 2030, the atmospheric conditions were similar to those of September 9th, 1904 so we agreed I'd try to go back in time and stop him from starting that life."

He nodded, and she picked up the salad, ready for the tiny circuit of the room.

"I broke into the Master Suite, exactly as Henry described it, arriving in 1904, and a year later I thought I'd done the job.

"Then on August 30, 1905, the conditions were similar again.

"During a thunderstorm, I was in the Master Suite when I somehow phase shifted. I was there, but no one could see me."

She took a shuddery breath, rubbed her eyes that had started to water, and sat down again with a thud.

"Except Dante. Did you happen to find a dog anywhere?"

"I'm sorry."

"Poor Dante. He was a good dog. I'm going to miss him."

She wrestled for control of herself, and largely succeeded.

"Then I met a guy called Zoo, who said the date was December 17 2066. There was a thunder storm, and he said something about gravity before he disappeared.

"Or maybe I disappeared," she waved an arm around the room, "and arrived here."

Kumahl leaned forward, "so what was the date you left?"

"August 30, 1905"

"So, for you, time didn't move, but outside of you, time continued to pass. What about Henry?"

"Zoo said Henry disappeared in 1922, but I don't know anything about the circumstances."

Morag was suddenly exhausted, "I feel like this has been the longest day of my existence. I need a nap."

Kumahl jumped to his feet and waggled his phone at her. I've got enough to get started with some research, so I'll let you sleep, and come back later.

Which was a little funny, because that was almost the same as she'd told Henry, whenever that was.

《《 • 》》

As he made his way to the Lab, Kumahl was excited by the puzzle. Seemingly she'd been the victim of some kind of cosmic event, but how?

Was it the eclipse? What was it about the passage of the moon between the earth and the sun? Fluctuating atmospheric conditions?

Was it the weather? Particularly a massive injection of energy into the atmosphere via lightning.

Was there a gravity well? You need a lot of energy to escape a gravity well. You'd need to calculate the energy expenditure against the gravity based on where you were and where you wanted to go.

Then you'd need to choose the kind of propellant, in this case lightning, so you could calculate how much propellant you needed.

But lightning's an unreliable energy source, with variances in voltage and current. The power is also brief but large; a 10-microsecond burst of 5 gigajoules would result in 500 terrawatts of power.

You could store some of the strike energy in a capacitor, but you'd need to shunt off everything that was so high it might damage the capacitor.

Then again, the energy of a lightning strike is often dissipated into the atmosphere before it hits the ground.

Theoretically, you could draw lighting with a laser induced plasma channel, though you'd need a lot of energy to pull the lightning in.

So, there was a more or less obvious link between the lightning and a potential gravity well, but what was the significance of the total eclipse? Was it something to do with the moon's ascending node?

It seemed significant that it had all occurred in the same place, so his first step was to check the history of Hayward Hall.

Incredibly, the property was still there, only now it was a kind of psychic retreat and training centre with an on-site observatory.

The original core of the house was still there, surrounded by small accommodation units; scientists on one side, and psychics on the other.

He checked through the registry of owners, noting the transfer of ownership through the Foxes to the renowned astrophysicist Dr Paul Maidenwell, and on to the Maidenwell Trust.

In fact, Maidenwell had gone some way towards reclaiming the original grounds before he died, leaving a dedicated fund in his estate to continue the purchases.

What the hell had happened there?

It seemed Dr Paul Maidenwell had once been the host of a show called *The Ghost Detectors*, under the name Zoo, and during filming of the last episode he'd fallen through the ceiling and been injured quite severely.

After the show he'd bought the house and turned it into a business; initially as a haunted house theme park and later as the psychic retreat.

Before he died, he'd transferred the house into a trust with all his other assets and left it to be run as a going concern.

Now that he'd met Morag, he understood the stipulation the Master Suite remained unused; it was a sensible precaution to prevent anyone else being cast adrift in time and space.

Or perhaps, somehow preventing her return.

It seemed that after his encounter with Morag, he'd studied astrophysics under his real name; Dr Paul Maidenwell. He'd been one of the pioneers of research into special relativity.

And if Maidenwell had been focused on finding a way to bring her back...

Well, that was excellent; he could take it up where Maidenwell left off.

But out of curiosity, he calculated the earth standard date the container arrived, for Melbourne Australia. February 21, 2157.

He checked all the dates she'd given him:

- September 9, 1904, the date Morag arrived - total eclipse in the Saros cycle.
- August 30, 1905, the date Morag phase shifted - total solar eclipse in the Inex series.
- 1922, the date Henry disappeared - he'd wager that one would be September 21, another total eclipse in the Saros cycle.
- November 25, 2030, the date Morag went back to 1904 - total eclipse in the Saros cycle.
- December 17 2066, the date Dr Maidenwell met Morag - total eclipse in the Saros cycle.

- February 21, 2157, the date she's arrived in the container - total eclipse in the Saros cycle.

It was pretty coincidental that almost all the eclipses were Saros cycle but why was the phase shift an Inex cycle?

And why didn't any of the other Inex cycle dates trigger shifts?

Unless they did, but she was alone and didn't notice them?

The next date in the Saros cycle was February 21, 2175. The cycle started July 13 1219, lasting through to September 5, 2499.

Was it reasonable to assume she couldn't go further forward than 2499? That if she was before 1219 or after 2499, she would be safe?

Ack.

He needed to do something physical to make his brain move, so he booked an exercise pod with a treadmill.

But before he left the lab, he set off a computer programme to look for commonalities in the conditions on her dates.

And then to analyse all of the possible eclipses of any kind within the Saros date range, looking for additional dates with similarities.

As he ran, he considered the exercise pod; it was essentially an enclosure for a gravity field. Once closed, it could theoretically be relocated anywhere on the ship, but in practice, was suspended from the ceiling.

Could you rig one up as a kind of Faraday Cage to direct lightning away from a passenger, while using it as a method of propulsion? Like a kind of time capsule?

He abandoned the exercise pod, and jogged through the back passageways to the lab.

In a flow state, working through lunch, not noticing his hunger.

The computer had finished its analysis, returning a small set of variables that applied to each date.

In a few Earth days there was one date, out of sequence, with the right conditions.

So, the next thing to do was look at her physical conditions, starting with the subatomic scan.

Something about the phase shift had preserved her body's age in 1905. There were no signs of decay; she literally hadn't aged a day.

There was nothing to suggest she might experience rapid ageing on the other side, but it was a risk.

In fact, there was the potential that she would stay the same age forever.

Though it might be better to do a full set of medical diagnostics to see what they were working with.

He sent a brief report to the Captain on his findings so far, included a request for Morag to be given an internet accessible device, and the scans, as well as permission to begin fitting out a pod to send her home

Then he ate some lunch and organised a tray for Morag.

《《 • 》》

Morag was asleep, curled up on the bed like a cat.

"Morag," he called her name.

She didn't respond.

He called her name again, and touched her shoulder.

Still no response.

He shook her gently.

Still nothing.

He put a call into Chief Medical Officer Yang, who arrived moments later.

"What happened?" he asked.

"Nothing, that I know of.

"She took a shower, and ate a little breakfast this morning. She said she was tired, so I left her to sleep.

"That was about an hour after I left the Captain's Rooms this morning."

"All right," he pulled out his phone, "let's get rid of some of this furniture," he swiped his finger up and got rid of everything but the bed, which reverted back to a biobed.

He tapped a few times, and coloured lasers took the scans.

"This isn't looking good, there's been a deterioration in some of her core functions. I'll need to make some adjustments."

He tapped out a prescription in his phone, and swiped it towards the biobed, ejected a hypospray from the bed, and injected it into Morag's neck.

The scans continued; "it looks like some kind of time sickness. She's stabilising, but if she's going to survive, you'll need to send her back sooner rather than later."

Kumahl took a step back, "I've got an idea, but I can't do it for a couple of days, and I've no way of knowing whether it will work."

Yang put his hand on his hip, and gestured his phone at the bed. "She will die if she stays here. She might die when she goes back, but at least you'll know you did your best for her, so get to work."

Kumahl and Chief Medical Officer Yang laid the still comatose Morag, in the modified exercise pod and closed the lid.

The Captain, Security Chief Singh, and Chief of Logistics McMasters watched on.

They'd dressed her in the clothes she arrived with.

It felt cruel to let her go without saying something, or wishing her better, or giving her a small gift.

McMasters handed Kumahl the control mechanism, and as he activated the pod, the Captain said, "have a safe journey."

The pod disappeared with a sucking noise and a pop.

She was gone, and it was a moot point whether Kumahl would ever know what had happened to her.

He looked, but couldn't find any other references to her after her 2030 disappearance.

But Yang was right, he had done his best for her.

And earned a field promotion.

Morag landed with a thump.

The capsule fell open and she spilled out.

As lightening played over it, it fizzled and disintegrated.

She was found unconscious, deep in dense bushland, near Mount Donna Buang, East of Melbourne by bush walkers who called the Police.

The emergency services evacuated her by helicopter to the Royal Melbourne Hospital.

A small newspaper article mentioned the mystery woman who'd been discovered in bushland without her memory.

It was a sensational beat up with details of meteor showers and a supposed hovering UFO with allegations of alien abduction.

But Morag new better. She hadn't been abducted by aliens, but returned by Earthers from the future.

Not that she told anyone.
Ever.

THE END

ABOUT THE AUTHOR

Alexandria Blaelock writes stories, some of them for *Ellery Queen's Mystery Magazine* and *Pulphouse Fiction Magazine*. She's also written four self-help books applying business techniques to personal matters like getting dressed, cleaning house, and feeding your friends.

As a recovering Project Manager, she's probably too fond of sticking to plan. She lives in a forest because she enjoys birdsong, the scent of gum leaves and the sun on her face. When not telecommuting to parallel universes from her Melbourne based imagination, she watches K-dramas, talks to animals, and drinks Campari. At the same time.

Discover more at www.alexandriablaelock.com.

BOOKS BY
ALEXANDRIA BLAELOCK

SHORT STORY COLLECTIONS

The Histories of Hayward Hall
Lovelorn, Lovestruck and Love at First Sight
Common or Garden Variety Heroes
Case Files of the Wilkinson Detective Agency
Unavoidable Fates

OTHER FICTION

That Love Nonsense

MS BLAELOCK'S BOOKS

Stress Free Dinner Parties
Signature Wardrobe Planning
Holistic Personal Finance
Minimally Viable Housekeeping
Planning a Life Worth Living

www.ingramcontent.com/pod-product-compliance
Lightning Source LLC
Chambersburg PA
CBHW030814190726
48285CB00003B/1172